Famous Legends From Portugal

Miguel Carvalho Abrantes

This book was written with a significant problem in mind – if you're looking for information on famous myths and legends from Portugal, either you need to know the Portuguese language, or you're constantly faced with the exact same stories told in almost the exact same way. As such, you may find, if you search for them online, endless references to legends such as the Rooster of *Barcelos*[1] or the Miracle of the Roses, but you will hardly ever be told how popular those stories really are among natives, or that they are almost always presented in an incomplete form.

This book attempts to fix that whole problem by succinctly retelling $50+2$[2] of Portugal's most famous legends, selected in an unusual, yet unbiased and very significant way – in the middle of the XIX century, when the famous portuguese author *Teófilo Braga*, one of the first collectors of local tales and traditions, wrote his book *O Povo Portuguez nos seus Costumes, Crenças e Tradições*[3], he included in it a listing of the country's most famous stories of a legendary nature. And so, for this book I started by compiling all of those, then removing the very few stories which seem to have lost their importance across time (e.g. they referred to places that no longer exist and which people seem

---

1   In this book, whenever a word or phrase in Portuguese is mentioned, it is placed in *italics*, so the reader can know those are native words. Whenever a translation is important for the context, it'll be presented in a note such as this one too.

2   There is a bit of a funny story behind this number – although the original version was only going to feature 50 legends, preliminary readers noticed that two crucial stories were strangely absent from it. So, instead of removing a few legends just to add those additional ones, I felt it was better to simply add two more to the book.

3   I.e. "The Portuguese People in their Mores, Beliefs and Traditions". The work does not exist in English translation.

to have completely forgotten), adding a few notable references to more recent material of the legendary and mythic kind, and proceeded by including some brief personal comments regarding the cultural impact of some of these stories. Finally, I confronted other natives with the legends present here, to further assess how popular they are, and to attempt to locate other legends which could be missing here. And so, by proceeding in such a way, it is guaranteed that you are here going to read about THE most famous legends from Portugal, ones which were consistently remembered and retold across the centuries to our own day and age, instead of a merely personal collection of stories some random reader found specially enjoyable.

However, this book would not have been possible if it wasn't for the staff of the website Mitologia.pt . Although written almost completely in Portuguese, they've collected hundreds of myths and legends from all over the world, and many of the stories presented here were adapted – naturally, with the permission and blessing from them – for this English version, with the main intent of making those native stories also available to readers all over the world. And so, I have to deeply thank them for their work.

As always, I hope you enjoy this small book as much as I enjoyed compiling and editing it. Hopefully, it will make it possible for non-natives to access these legends for the very first time, since some of them are now obscure even in Portugal, and appear to have never been presented in English before.

Miguel Carvalho Abrantes

Index

Chapter I – Before Portugal was Portugal (Legends 1-7)

Although Portugal, as a completely independent country, was only born in the XII century AD, there are many local legends which directly or indirectly refer to a time period before the foundation of this nation by our first king, [*Dom*]⁴ *Afonso Henriques*. They range from legends coming from Ancient Greek and Latin sources, up to ones which were later retroactively associated with a time period in which the country wasn't born yet.

1- The Foundation of Lisbon by Ulysses

Perhaps the most famous of all ancient stories associated with the territory of Portugal is that of Lisbon's foundation by Ulysses, the roman name given to the hero of Homer's *Odyssey*. However, those who read Homer's poem looking for any evidence of this event will quickly find themselves frustrated – the episode does not appear in the epic at all, it is a late addition to the story, with authors from Ancient Greece and Rome, such as Strabo, always alluding to the legend in very general lines, essentially saying that the hero came to the coasts of Portugal at an undisclosed time during his travels and founded the city of *Olissipo* or "Ulyssipo" there, where he also built a temple to a goddess, frequently Tethys, by the seashore.

---

4   In Portuguese, also every king, lady and noble is usually referred to by the title *"Dom"* (or *"Dona"*, for the feminine), which essentially means "Lord". Those titles were usually omitted here, since they add nothing to the plot.

As you may suppose, Ulysses is a legendary figure and, as such, it is very unlikely he truly founded the city of Lisbon. However, across time many vestiges of a previous Roman occupation were found all over this city, with the most famous and impressive probably being a small theater renovated in Nero's time, i.e. during the first century of our era, which can still be found just near Saint George's Castle, between the *Rua de São Mamede* and the *Rua da Saudade*[5].

2- The Cavern of the Triton

Ancient authors, such as Pliny the Elder, also refer to the existence of a famous cavern, somewhere near the city of Lisbon, where a Triton – a half-man, half-fish deity – could often be heard playing his music.

Although the exact location of the original cavern is now completely unknown, across time people started to imagine it was somewhere near the shores of *Sintra*, and so you may be able to find this legend associated with multiple beaches and caverns near that village. But, perhaps even more importantly, if you ever visit the *Palácio da Pena*[6], you will be able to spot the "Triton Gateway" there,

---

5   These are the names of two streets in Lisboa. If you go to where they intersect, you're able to see the ancient theatre there, for free.

6   Or Palace of the *Pena*, in its English form. Although *pena* usually means "feather" in Portuguese, it should be noted that there is no noteworthy legend associating any feathers with the place; instead, the word is a corrupted form of *penha*, or "rock", over the fact the palace, and a previous monastery which once occupied the same place, was built on

the presence of the statue naturally attesting this legend's significant popularity across the centuries.

3- *Guesto Ansures*

Legend has it that around the VIII and IX centuries AD a muslim ruler of Cordoba instituted a rule according to which 100 beautiful virgins from his domains had to be delivered to him every year. The horrible tradition went on for many years, until a young woman from Portugal was picked. Some claim her name was *Sancha*, while others say she was *Mécia*. When she, along with five other companions, was being escorted by many Moors to what would one day be Spain, they all stopped near a place where many fig trees could be found.

The six ladies cried and cried over their fate, until a mysterious knight showed up. Feeling compassion for them, he asked what was going on, revealed his name to be *Guesto Ansures*, and then fought the Moors in an attempt to save these ladies. He was a very powerful knight, and he defeated many opponents until his sword was eventually broken; then, he ripped a branch from a fig tree and continued his combat, using the branch as if it was a completely new sword. Sooner than later he defeated all the enemies and saved the ladies. He took the six of them back to their respective homes, but *Mécia*'s father was so happy with his daughter's safe return that he quickly allowed her to marry this powerful knight, and they later ended up having at least one

---

top of a very prominent cliff.

male child.

This legend is noteworthy for two reasons. There is an extant poem, usually titled *Canção do Figueiral*[7] and attributed to *Guesto Ansures* himself, which reports the main incident of the plot from a first-person perspective (although some studies consider it to be a XVI century forgery). Also, if you travel all over Portugal, you may eventually be able to spot a small village named *Figueiredo das Donas*[8]. From a tourist standpoint there is nothing specially noteworthy about the place, but it allegedly received its name over the fact this famous rescue of these six ladies by *Guesto Ansures* took place in the area nearby.

4- The mysterious *Marinha*

Once, as a noble man named *Froião* was hunting and passed by a beach, he saw a very beautiful woman sleeping by the sea shore. He felt desperately in love with her, but she never said a single word to him. So feeling no opposition to the whole idea from her, he took her to his home, baptized her under the christian name of *Marinha*[9], and they had multiple children. Then, one day, *Froião* playfully tried to throw one of his offspring to the fireplace. Visibly worried over the incident, the mother suddenly tried to shout, a mysterious slice of meat fell from

---

7   Or "Song of the Fig Orchard".
8   Or "Fig Orchard of the Ladies".
9   Literally "Marine", due to the fact she was found by the sea shore.

her mouth, and she was finally able to talk. The couple married soon after, and they were happy for many years.

Although modern retellings of this legend, originally designed to explain the origin of the family of the *Marinhos*, often call this *Marinha* a mermaid, it should be noted the original literary source, from the XIV century, simply alludes to her as a "marine woman". What this designation really means remains uncertain, but absolutely nothing in the plot indicates that she was not fully human in shape.

5- The Tower of the Frog

There was once a tower in the north of Portugal simply known as the "Tower of the Frog". It received its name over one *Florentim Barreto*, a noble who used to live there and imposed many brutal rules to those living nearby, including a right of *prima nocte* on all marriages[10]. Due to all his constant misdeeds, and perhaps also because he was specially ugly, he was nicknamed "the frog". However, his misdeeds went on and on, until some people approached an undisclosed monarch and asked him for permission to kill, literally, "a frog who raped many young women." It is unknown if the king found the request odd or funny, but he gave his permission, and so people killed *Florentim Barreto* without fearing any penalties, effectively ending his

---

10 Basically, after people were married, but before they were able to consummate that action, he reserved for himself the right of having sex with the bride before her husband ever did.

horrible actions once and for all.

Today, you can still find a *Quinta da Torre de Dom Sapo* where the tower once stood, near the city of *Viana do Castelo*, but in the name of progress the original structure was demolished in the XIX century, and so only a very faint memory of this legend seems to remain.

6- *João de Montemor*

In the IX century a man who became famous as *Abbot João* lived near the city of *Coimbra*. He was a very faithful and religious man, and when he noticed a very young orphan abandoned in the street, he received him in his home and raised him as if he was his own son, going as far as naming him *Garcia Eanes*. However, for unknown reasons this young man later left his adoptive family and joined the Moors, adopting for himself the name of *Zulema*.

As the years went by, these enemies of the Christian faith conquered many lands, eventually reaching the area near *Montemor*, where both *João* and *Zulema* once lived. Their army was extremely large, and so the locals were certain they could not win the battle. As such, hoping to spare their love ones of a terribly fate, they decided to kill all the women and children before joining the battlefield one final time. In the fierce combat that ensued *João* ultimately defeated *Zulema* (versions diverge in whether he killed him or not), and if the locals did not manage to defeat all the enemies, at least they were able to make them flee. And then, when they got back to *Montemor*, a miracle happened – perhaps because these men had fought on the side of the Christian faith, all the women and children had been brought back to life!

The city of *Montemor-o-Velho*[11], where these events are alleged to have taken place, still exists today, and you can visit its castle. The place of the victory of *Abade João* and his army is still known, since the chapel of *Nossa Senhora de Ceiça* was erected there, and despite the fact it was extensively remodeled multiple times across the centuries, inside of it you can still find many notable references to this legendary battle and its main hero, locally known as *Abade João*.

7- *Gaia*, or King *Ramiro*

King *Ramiro II*, native of Léon, lived in the first half of the X century. He was already married to one *Aldora,* but later fell in love with a princess of Muslim origin. Naturally, her brother *Alboazer* did not allow her to marry someone who was both already married and a Christian, and so *Ramiro* ended up kidnapping her, later baptizing her with the Christian name of *Artiga*. Naturally upset over the whole incident, *Alboazer* in return kidnapped *Aldora, Ramiro*'s first wife, among many other people of her court, and took them all to his castle in

---

11   There is another city named *Montemor* in Portugal, in the area of the *Alentejo,* but this legend clearly refers to the city near *Coimbra*. Across the centuries they became known respectively as *Montemor-o-Novo* and *Montemor-o-Velho,* so they could be easily distinguished from each other.

the city of *Gaia*.

Ramiro, hoping to rescue them all, prepared his army, told them to wait for a sign, and entered the city disguised as a beggar. He found his queen, but she – now in love with her gentle kidnapper – betrayed him to the moor king. And so, as he was about to be killed, he asked for a final wish, the one of blowing his horn. Such favor was granted, and when he blew his horn his armies understood it as the promised sign – they quickly attacked the city, defeating all their enemies and rescuing the people who had been kidnapped.

As everyone was making their way back home, *Ramiro* noticed his (first) wife was crying over *Alboazer's* death. She had fallen in love with him. Disgusted, her husband fastened her to a millstone and threw her into the ocean, so killing her. Then, he lived the rest of his life with his beloved *Artiga*.

Unfortunately, the city now known as *Vila Nova de Gaia*, near *Porto*, no longer has a castle, but this legend still appears to be widely known in the north of Portugal. In fact, *Ramiro* blowing his horn can still be seen in the same city's coat of arms[12]!

---

12 For this and similar instances in this book, you can go to a search engine and type a phrase like "*brasão de* [name of the town here]", the images should reveal the information stated here even if you don't speak the original language.

Chapter II – The Time of *Afonso Henriques* (8-13)

Portugal's very first king, in the XII century, was *Afonso Henriques*, and to this day popular tradition attributes to him many legendary feats. In fact, when I was a child my grandfather used to tell me someone once opened the king's grave, located in *Coimbra*, and noticed his sword was so large and heavy that he could easily kill 10 men with a single blow. Although such story was, in itself, a pure legend, it still shows how to this day the first king, surnamed *O Conquistador*[13], is considered to have been able to perform absolutely impossible feats of strength. As such, there are many legends associated with his time and his many conquests, of which the ones reported here are the most famous.

8- The Curse of *Teresa*

There is a famous episode in Portugal's history which says that *Afonso Henriques* once fought against his own mother, *Teresa*, for possession of Portugal. Even back in school, when we first learn about this, it conjures the idea they fought against each other physically[14], but it is more likely that their respective armies did all the fighting for them, until the mother's was eventually defeated by his son's. However, a significant addition to the story states that *Afonso Henriques* eventually captured his mother and took her with him wherever he

---

13 Or "the Conqueror".
14 It is often said that the king *bateu na mãe,* i.e. "hit his mother".

went, always keeping her imprisoned as if she was a mere criminal. Eventually fed up with this horrible act, Teresa cursed his own child, explicitly wishing that he would break his leg. He later ended up breaking it during a siege to the city of Badajoz, and he never walked again.

9- The Black Bishop

From a religious standpoint, the fact *Afonso Henriques* had imprisoned his own mother was extremely shocking. So, the Pope ordered the king to release her, and the bishop of *Coimbra* further emphasized this order, under the penalty of excommunication. The king refused to listen to either of them, and instead decided to select a new bishop for the city, but everyone refused that honor. So, he ordered *Suleima*, a black priest, to take the empty spot, which horrified many of the local people[15]. For this action the entire kingdom of Portugal was excommunicated, and remained so until the king threatened another papal legate and, supposedly but not certainly, released his mother *Teresa* from prison, effectively ending their long feud.

Today, it is unknown if the events regarding this "Black Bishop" truly took place, since the records from the See of *Coimbra* do not contain anyone with such an unusual name, but in the XIX century the writer *Alexandre Herculano* wrote a fictional version of this legend,

---

15 It should be noted that the whole problem was not the colour of his skin, but the fact he was a former muslim, as his name clearly indicates.

perhaps adding more details to the original story.

10- *Geraldo Sem Pavor*

A few years after Lisbon was taken from the Moors, *Afonso Henriques* found himself near what is now the city of *Évora*. A powerful castle surrounded it, and the place seemed very difficult to conquer. And so, one of his knights, who had previously committed a crime and now sought the king's forgiveness, had an idea – originally named *Geraldo Geraldes*, he suggested infiltrating the city and opening the gates from the inside. The king considered this to be a very risky plan, but he allowed *Geraldo* to follow through with it.

The knight disguised himself in some way – different versions state he took either the form of a beggar or a troubadour – and explored the city's defenses. When he noticed that the local king lived in a certain tower, he waited for night time and then climbed it all the way to the top. He killed the king's daughter, who was watching over the city, and then murdered the sleeping king, before stealing the keys to the city. With them, he was finally able to open the gates, allowing his army to come in and quickly defeat the Moors. For these actions he started being known as *Geraldo Sem Pavor*[16], and from then on *Afonso Henriques* forgave his past misdeeds and made him the mayor of the recently-conquered city.

---

16 Or "Fearless Geraldo".

Although this whole legend is specially famous around *Évora*, in *Alentejo*, where you can still see the knight and the heads of two Moors in the city's coat of arms, you may be able to find streets and locations all over Portugal sharing his unusual name, since many oral traditions associate him with other minor events from the time of the same national king.

11- *Egas Moniz*

Egas Moniz is commonly known as *Afonso Henriques'* preceptor, and multiple legends connect the two, but one of them is specially famous above all others. In it, *Egas Moniz* is stated to have promised to *Afonso VII*, king of Léon and Castile, that the then-king of Portugal was going to give up his land and become a vassal of his'. However, when *Afonso Henriques* later decided he was not going to fulfill this promise after all, *Egas Moniz* felt his own reputation was on the line. As such, he traveled to the domains of *Afonso VII* along with the rest of his family, each member carrying a noose around their neck, and they all deposited their lives in the hands of the foreign monarch. The spanish king was so impressed with this honorable action that he completely forgave the apparent misdeed, and soon after these events the preceptor came back to Portugal unharmed.

Although this legendary episode is portrayed in many places, if you ever go to the train station of *São Bento*, in the city of *Porto*, you'll be able to see some tiles representing the beautiful moment in which *Egas Moniz* presented himself and his family to the king of Léon and Castile.

12- The Miracle of *Ourique*

The most famous of all legends associated with *Afonso Henriques* is certainly the one of the Miracle of *Ourique*. The kernel of the plot was significantly changed across the centuries, but in its most famous version we are told that in 1139 the portuguese king found himself in the battlefield, about to face thousands of Moors, the combined armies of five kings. He had very little hope for victory, until a mysterious man entered his tent during the night and invited him to come outside. When the king did so, he looked at the sky and saw an image of a crucified Jesus Christ in it, accompanied by an endless multitude of angels. Then, Christ talked to *Afonso Henriques* – the words spoken at the time varied widely across the centuries, from one report to another – and promised him the victory, while he also prophesied the future and awarded endless glory to the future kingdom of Portugal.

Afonso Henriques ended up winning this battle against the seemingly impossible odds, and as a result he added five blue shields – one for each king of the Moors he defeated at that time – to his coat of arms, which can still be seen in Portugal's flag to this day.

Although some people tend to consider that Portugal was only born after this battle, as a divinely-ordained kingdom endorsed by Jesus Christ, it should again be noted that this one legend was significantly altered and improved across the centuries, essentially to make it seem like the country was truly fated to exist and to become the greatest empire in the world. This would later lead to one of Portugal's most famous legends, but that's a matter for another chapter.

13- Two legends of the conquest of Lisbon

When Lisbon was finally conquered from the Moors, which occurred in 1147, this generated many legends. To tell them all in this section would be a very difficult task, and so I decided to select two of the most famous ones, which are still very present in the same city today.

Martim Moniz[17] was one among many knights who was helping *Afonso Henriques* conquer the city. At one point he noticed that a very important door to the castle was about to be closed, and so he stopped that action with his own body, placing it in such a way that it would be impossible to close the gate. Taking advantage of this, the Christians were then able to easily enter the castle, and the now-dead knight was honored as a true hero. And so, nowadays, if you visit the subway station that goes under this hero's name, you'll be able to see many

---

17 Seemingly unrelated to the *Egas Moniz* mentioned above, despite their common surname.

figures from the conquest of Lisbon there – and if you play close attention to all of them, you may even be able to spot this hero stuck between two doors, the closure of which is represented with two white arrows pointing in opposite directions.

Another legend from the same period refers to a knight simply known as *Henrique*, who died under unknown circumstances during the siege of the city. He was buried in a new church, and he unexpectedly started performing miracles – he healed some guards who were deaf and mute, appeared in people's dreams requesting reburials for his former companions, and, perhaps the most famous of them all, made a palm tree miraculously grow in his grave. The branches of the latter were quickly taken away by pilgrims, possibly because they were attributed to have miraculous properties, until the whole tree even disappeared (or, according to another version, was stolen by pilgrims during the night). However, the *Rua da Palma*[18], in the same city, still preserves a notable reference to this whole legend, either because pilgrims seeking *Henrique*'s grave usually rested there, or because it once contained a palm tree which descended from this miraculous one.

---

18 Or "Street of the Palm[tree]".

Chapter III – The Portuguese Against the Moors (14-17)

Although there are some portuguese legends which pit older Christians against the Moors, as we've already seen in the first chapter, the most popular type of legend in Portugal is arguably the one in which late Portuguese knights fight against Moors. There is an almost endless number of legends following that basic scheme, frequently presenting a princess falling in love with a knight and later converting to Christianity, or with the overall intention of explaining the name of a certain location. As such, you can see a few examples in this chapter.

14- *Moura Salúquia*

Salúquia was a princess who practiced the religion of Islam, and she was the daughter of a governor of a city in *Alentejo*, which possibly went by the original names of "Arucitana" or "Ilmanijah". She fell in love with *Bráfama*, a notable man who lived in the town of *Aroche*, not very far away from her own. One day, Christians killed her lover, took his clothes, and one of the knights dressed them in order to pretend he was the princess' lover. When she saw "him" approaching the city – some versions even add this happened in her wedding day, further explaining her eagerness – she ordered the opening of the doors, and so the Christians quickly approached and easily conquered the city. *Salúquia*, realizing what her pure love for a man had caused, killed herself by jumping from the city's highest tower.

The village of *Moura* supposedly got its name over this whole occurrence[19], and to this day *Salúquia*'s dead body, lying in front of the tower, can still be seen in its coat of arms. Also, if you ever visit this place, a tower, supposedly the one associated with the legend, can still be found there.

15- *Alenquer*

In the coat of arms of the village of *Alenquer* you may see a dog in front of a castle (or near a tree, if you spot an older version). According to this legend, back in the time of the Moors there was here a dog named *Alão*, who was in charge of protecting the city. However, there are at least two main versions of the events which ensued.

According to the first, this animal constantly kept the key to the gates with him, and so the conquerors sort of seduced him by recurring to a bitch. The other states that this dog barked whenever enemies were approaching, so warning the dwellers of the castle, and in order to avoid this the conquerors approached him near a stream, in very playful ways, and the animal ended up not barking at all.

Either way, *Afonso Henriques* and his companions so conquered this animal and the king then said "*Alão quer*"[20] – i.e. the animal supposedly desired either the bitch, or the conquest of the city by the Christians – which was across time corrupted to the current name of

---

19 *Moura* is the name given to a female moor.
20 I.e. "Alão desires".

this village. However, it should also be noted this village no longer has a castle today, since it was heavily damaged across the centuries and never repaired at all, given the fact it lost its defensive value early on.

16- *Traga-Mouros*

Although this legend is now known under many different names, its plot is generally the same. One *Gonçalo Hermingues*, also known as *Traga-Mouros*[21] over his ferocity against the Moors, fell in love with a princess named *Fátima*. Given their religions, and in spite of the princess' truly requited love, her father would never allow them to marry, and so *Gonçalo* kidnapped her during a festivity. A fight ensued, in which this hero even killed the princess' father. She later converted to Christianity, was given the new name of *Ouroana* or *Oriana*, and married this man she loved so much.

If you travel through Portugal you'll be able to notice two towns separated by a small distance, one of them named *Fátima* (best known for the appearances of the Virgin Mary in the XX century), and the other called *Ourém*. According to popular belief, the former was where this couple lived before they got married, while the latter was where they moved to after the princess' conversion and marriage.

---

21 Or "Moor Crusher".

17- The Conquest of *Silves*

Taking the city of *Silves*, in the Algarve, from the Moors was no easy task, but there is a little quaint legend related to it. It says that *Branca*, a daughter of king *Afonso III*, once fell in love with an islamic man who possessed two magical branches given to him by a fairy – one of myrtle and one of laurel, as symbols of love and glory – and he was advised to always follow their command.

For many years *Branca* and this man lived their passion, and his branch of myrtle was completely green, while the one of laurel had apparently withered. However, as time went on, since they could never marry, the foreign warrior eventually moved to *Silves*. Then, when the city was conquered by the Christians, and this combatant was killed, something quite unusual was noticed by the conquerors – one of the deceased had two small branches in his hand, one of myrtle, which was completely withered, and one of laurel, which still flourished. He had lost love, but by dying in the city he obtained endless glory, and he is still remembered today.

In the current form, this is clearly a late legend – medieval Portuguese stories rarely feature fairies and such extensive magical elements as are presented here – but it is also such a quaint plot that it had to be retold in these lines.

Chapter IV – Legends of Other Kings (18-24)

Although *Afonso Henriques* is likely the most prolific king when it comes to legendary material, in Portugal there are also many legends associated with other kings. The legends presented in this chapter are ones in which those monarchs have a significant role, even if they're not always the main hero.

18- *Maria Pais Ribeira* (and *Sancho I*)

Maria Pais Ribeira was a mistress of king *Sancho I*, in the XII century, and they had multiple children together. When the king died, she tried to quickly retreat to the lands he had offered her, but she ended up being kidnapped by one *Gomes Lourenço de Alvarenga*, who had a massive, but also completely unrequited, love for her. He took her to Castile, i.e. today a part of Spain, so hoping to make her rescue by the Portuguese much more difficult. But she was a wise woman – eventually faking her passion for the kidnapper, she pretended to want to marry him in her own lands, and to do so they had to return to Portugal. When they did so, *Maria Pais Ribeira* asked *Afonso II*, the son of *Sancho I* and new king of Portugal, to avenge the whole kidnapping, which he quickly granted. Finally free from harm, she ended up marrying another man, one she actually loved, and in her old age joined a monastery.

19- *Martim de Freitas* (plus *Sancho II* and *Afonso III*)

In the early XIII century the king *Sancho II* needed a mayor for the city of *Coimbra*, at the time still protected by a very strong and well-positioned castle. He picked a noble man named *Martim de Freitas*, who promised him his complete fidelity. So, the city was completely invincible for many years, even after a long siege, and the mayor performed his job in an absolutely perfect way.

Then, he heard that his king had died, and that he should surrender the city to a new monarch, *Afonso III*. He was unsure if these news were actually true, or if they were part of a plan to invade the city. So, he obtained a safe-conduct and traveled all the way to Toledo, in Spain, to be able to see the deceased body of his king. When he noticed that *Sancho II* was really dead, he deposited the key to *Coimbra*'s doors in the deceased's hands, quickly took it back, and then delivered it in the hands of *Afonso III*, the next king of Portugal, as if to say that he had successfully completed his task and passed the city along to the new monarch.

Today *Coimbra* no longer has a noticeable castle, most of the remaining parts of its wall having been demolished in the XX century, and so its once-imposing gates are left to the visitor's imagination, but if you travel there and look closely you may still be able to spot, here and there, some remnants of its medieval fortifications, such as multiple towers and the *Palácio de Sobre-Ribas*.

20- The Punishment of the Bishop (and *Pedro I*[22])

The king *Pedro I* was specially famous for his keen sense of justice, leading people to surname him both *O Justiceiro* and *O Cruel*[23]. As such, when he heard that a certain bishop from the city of *Porto* was repeatedly having casual sex with a married woman, he decided he had to intervene and punish the misdeed by himself. As such, he invited the religious man to join him in a private place; then, he asked his personal entourage to close all the doors and windows, allowing the two to talk with complete privacy; finally, when he was completely alone with this bishop, he took off his regal clothes, ordered his visitor to remove his religious outfit, and then repeatedly hit him with a whip. The bishop would have died that day, if it wasn't for the fact the doors were eventually opened and a scribe of the monarch, who was also a friend to him, quickly advised him not to solve the problem in such a way... the legend does not preserve what happened afterwards, but one certainly has to assume the (always unnamed) religious man was scared so much by this whole occurrence that he mended his ways once and for all.

---

22 This same king is better known for his very famous love story with *Inês de Castro*. Although it is not retold in this chapter, you can find it in this book's final chapter.

23 i.e. "The Justicer" and "The Cruel", the second name coming from the fact his sense of justice was by some considered almost too strict, as you'll be able to see in the two legends present in this chapter.

21- The *Rousada* of *Benfica* (and *Pedro I*[24])

If you are into european football, chances are that you may have already heard about a team from Portugal succinctly named *Benfica*. While the real origin of this name, shared both by the club and an area of Lisbon where the team itself is based, remains unknown to this day, a few legends attempted to explain it, and this once-famous story is one of them.

As the king *Pedro I* was traveling in the area of Lisbon, he heard people talking about one "*Rousada*". Recognizing it as a very strange nickname for someone – the word isn't used any more, but at the time it meant "raped" – he inquired about it and learned about a woman named *Maria*, who had been raped by a man when she was still unmarried. In all honesty it should be noted they later married, and even had a very happy life together, but disgusted by the man's previous actions, the king ordered him to be hanged for his crime, going as far as telling Maria she "*bem fica*"[25] without him. Then, across time and in popular belief, the two words became connected, and they supposedly led to the current name of this area of Lisbon.

22- The Holy Queen and the Miracle of the Roses (and *Dinis*)

It is perhaps one of the most famous legends of Portugal,

---

24 Here, it should be noted that some versions associated this legend with a different monarch, such as *João I*.
25 I.e. "Stays well" or "will be well".

although specially associated with the city of *Coimbra*, where the "Holy Queen" *Isabel*'s tomb can still be visited today. There are many miracles associated with her in popular tradition, some of them more famous than others, including many other versions of this specific story[26], but the one reported here is undoubtedly the most well-known of those versions.

Legend has it that king *Dinis* did not want his queen to associate with the poor and needy, and so he repeatedly tried to stop her from doing so. Once, as she was about to distribute pieces of bread among those who were starving, her liege caught her in the act and angrily asked her what she was transporting inside her dress. Her answer became very famous all across Portugal – "*São rosas, Senhor, são rosas.*"[27] Still not convinced of the truth of her words, and even completely baffled at the whole idea that roses would even grow during winter time, the king then forced her to show him what she was carrying, and by a divine miracle the original loaves were turned into roses.

Although this whole legend and its many versions are, as already mentioned before, very famous in Portugal, the location where these events supposedly took place is now unknown – some associate it with *Coimbra*, a city specially linked to this *Isabel*, but you may also find it

---

26 Overall, those legends present the king confronting this queen with one of her attempts to help the poor, and some kind of miracle ensues, in which her good deeds are then hidden from the monarch.

27 I.e. "They're roses, my lord, they're roses."

in connection with cities such as *Alenquer*, *Leiria* or *Sabugal*, among others linked to her historical events and life.

23- The Magpies of *Sintra* (and *João I*)

If you ever visit the palace of the village of *Sintra*, the one with two large white chimneys, you will find in it a room in which the ceiling is decorated with many painted magpies, all of them accompanied by the text "*Por Bem*"[28]. Legend has it that the king *João I* was once in this palace and gave a small kiss to a lady of the court; his queen heard it taking place and later confronted the king with his action, leading him to utter those two words.

Why the magpies were painted in this palace remains unsure to this day, but chances are that the small episode took place in that specific room, and that the occurrence led to so much chatter that people spreading it were eventually equated to magpies, birds generally considered to talk a lot. And, if you have the opportunity of visiting this palace, be sure to also pay a significant look to a room containing many coats of arms – they represent the 72 noble families historically attested in Portugal[29].

---

28 It is not easy to translate the original expression in context, but overall it may have meant "without malice."

29 Technically they are now just 71, following the removal of the *Távoras*, for reasons that will be explained in another chapter.

24- The Return of King *Sebastião*, and the *Quinto Império*

This is arguably one of Portugal's most important legends, even if it is severely compressed nowadays. In fact, these events are repeatedly referenced in foggy mornings, where people still frequently, but now also jokingly, ask if the king may finally be coming back in that particular day. However, to fully understand this legend we have to travel back a few centuries into the past.

King *Sebastião* lived in the second half of the XVI century, when Portugal held a very large and rich ultramarine empire. Then, when he decided to invade the north of Africa, he suffered a very decisive loss at the battle of Battle of Alcácer Quibir and he mysteriously disappeared. Did he somehow escape the carnage, or did he die in that final battlefield? In Portugal, at the time, there were people who defended both opinions – some believed he would one day return, while others thought he was really dead, never to return again. The former soon led to something called *Sebastianismo*, the general idea that the king was hidden in a mysterious island and would one day return[30], a possibility further supported by many prophets who rose at the time (*Bandarra* undoubtedly being the most famous), and extended even more by the eventual appearance of many different people who pretended to be the missing king. Overall, many, many legends rose from this *Sebastianismo*, but they were also forgotten across time – now, people only tend to remember that he was supposed to come back

---

30 This point will be further talked about in one of the next chapters.

in a foggy morning, but the legend is no longer taken seriously.

But why was it ever taken seriously, you could be wondering? The idea dates all the way back to the "Miracle of *Ourique*", a famous legend which was already retold in a previous chapter. Assuming that whole miracle as true, believing that Jesus Christ really appeared to *Afonso Henriques* and promised him an endless and supreme empire for Portugal – the fifth major empire of this world[31], which is here called the *Quinto Império* – people thought that *Sebastião* could not be dead, or else that destiny would not be accomplished, since Spain was about to conquer Portugal – and, in fact, between 1581 and 1640 the country even had three spanish rulers. And so, chances are that the whole legend rose out of people's pure desperation, of their need to believe in "something" that kept them going through very hard times.

As you may suppose through this whole monologue, king *Sebastião* hasn't returned, at least not until now. Some say he is buried in the *Mosteiro dos Jerónimos*, in Lisbon, while others claim those are just somebody else's remains, collected randomly from the fields of Alcácer Quibir. The actual facts behind the legend are, however, much simpler – with the king's disappearance Portugal quickly started losing its vast wealth and ultramarine empire, never to recover either of the two. And so, to hope for his safe return is the same as wanting to expect a national return to that great empire we once had.

---

31 The previous four are generally taken to be Babylonia, Persia, Ancient Greece and Rome.

Chapter V – Legends of *Aljubarrota* (25-29)

Across the centuries Spain tried to invade Portugal multiple times. They were generally defeated, as you can easily infer from the fact the two countries are still independent from each other today, but the most famous of those confrontations was certainly the Battle of *Aljubarrota*, which took place in 1385. The historical event, in itself, generated many legends, of which I present the most notable ones here, preceded by a slightly earlier, but equally notable, legend of an invasion by the Spanish.

25- The Castle of *Faria*

A few years before the battle of *Aljubarrota* the Spanish tried to invade the north of Portugal. They conquered many lands until they eventually reached a small castle in the area of *Faria*, near the city of *Barcelos*. One *Nuno Gonçalves de Faria*, the castle's mayor, tried to stop the invasion with his small army, but he ultimately failed and was even captured. However, he was not defeated yet – he asked to talk to the people inside the castle, allegedly to convince them to give up that location without any physical confrontation, and he was allowed to. However, when he then talked to his own son, *Gonçalo Nunes de Faria*, he instead told him never to give up that castle, and to protect it with his own life. For his betrayal, this *Nuno* was then instantly killed by the Spanish, but through his heroic advice the castle of *Faria* was never conquered, and the whole invasion was soon repelled.

Today, only a very small part of the original castle of *Faria* remains, but a few years ago a small plaque was placed nearby, celebrating these legendary events, and particularly the honourable actions of this *Nuno Gonçalves de Faria*.

26- The Sword of the *Condestável*

The main general of the battle of *Aljubarrota* was a man named *Nuno Álvares Pereira*, who is best known in the culture of Portugal simply as the *Condestável*[32]. There are many stories and legends associated with him, but the one retold here appears to have been specially noteworthy across the centuries.

Once, when this *Nuno Álvares Pereira* was still young, he was in the area of *Ourém* and needed to sharpen one of his swords. He approached a certain *Fernão Vaz*, a swordsmith, who did the whole work for free, before stating that the future hero could pay whatever he wanted when he ended up becoming count of that city. These were possibly interpreted by the hero as strange words, until, many years later, the man then already known as the *Condestável* actually became the count of that city. By then *Fernão Vaz* had been accused of a crime he did not commit and condemned to death. In complete desperation, he

---

32 Although *Condestável* means "*constable*", in Portugal when it is not used as a title (e.g. "Constable John"), it refers almost exclusively to this historical figure.

asked for the local count's help. *Nuno* was called. Recognizing his former helper, he remembered the old debt and saved the old swordsmith, even obtaining a full pardon for him.

Although, as already aforementioned, there are many other legends associated with the *Condestável*, across the centuries he became specially famous as the protector of Portugal and a saint[33]; it was perhaps also his religious fervor which led him to join the *Convento do Carmo*, in Lisbon, later in his life.

27- *Ala dos Namorados* and *Doze de Inglaterra*

The Portuguese managed to win the battle of *Aljubarrota* through what was called the "tactic of the square". Fully describing it goes beyond this book's goal – in fact, almost everyone in Portugal would be unable to – but the name itself shows that the troops were somehow ordered in a square formation. This is notable because one of the laterals – whether the right, or left one, depends on the literary source you consult – became famous as the *Ala dos Namorados*[34]. This name comes from the fact it was composed almost exclusively by young and unmarried men, some of which were battling not only for their country, but also for the love they had for some woman – and moved by that double passion, they won the battle.

---

33 In case you are wondering, he only became an official saint for the Vatican in 2009.
34 Literally "Wing of the Boyfriends". The reasons for this are explained next.

But their story was not over yet. A few years later twelve ladies from England were insulted by twelve knights from that same country. Unable to obtain any help in their native land, they begged the Portuguese for help, since there was an alliance between the two countries. Twelve knights, ones who were originally part of the *Ala dos Namorados*, were selected for the job, and 11 of them departed by sea, while one of them, the most famous and usually known as *Magriço*, traveled by land and went through many adventures. Eventually, they all reunited in England – *Magriço* was almost too late for the tournament, deeply worrying his companions – and defeated all the 12 English knights, avenging the honor of the ladies who had requested their services.

Although these two legends are now not as widely known as they once were, to the point of being referenced in *Camões' Lusíadas*, they still remain significant in popular culture. For example, the *Ala dos Namorados* is also the name of a music band from Portugal, and when the Portuguese national football team went to play in the World Cup of England, in 1966, they chose for their name *"os Magriços"*, in an evident connection to the famous hero from the legend.

28- The Female Baker of *Aljubarrota*

The most famous legend associated with *Aljubarrota* is undoubtedly the one of a female baker widely known as *Brites de*

Almeida. According to her story, at one point the battle was going so badly for the Spanish that many of their soldiers tried to run away and hide in various places. Oddly, some of them decided to hide inside a big baker's oven, hoping to escape with their lives (or at least get some free bread). When this *Brites* noticed that seven men were hiding there, she got her baker's paddle and used it to hit them all so many times, and so hard, that she killed them all.

Although it is now unknown if this was a real historical event or a pure legend attempting to show that even women did their part in the famous battle, *Brites de Almeida*, the *Padeira de Aljubarrota*, is arguably the most famous heroine of Portuguese history, to the point late literary works even tried to add a (fictional) backstory to her life. Regardless of her historicity, if you ever go to *Aljubarrota* you are bound to find many references to this legend, as her personal bravery seems to have transcended the battle itself.

29- The Dome of *Batalha*

In Portugal, "*batalha*", as a single word, is almost synonymous with *Aljubarrota*. And so, after this famous victory, king *João I* ordered that a monastery should be built to celebrate the occurrence, as he had vowed to. The actual building process of the place now known as the *Mosteiro da Batalha*[35] took a significantly long time, but there is a

---

35 *Batalha*, or "battle", here taking a double sense, since it was built to celebrate the victory in the aforementioned battle, but also eventually originated a local city that goes by that

noteworthy legend associated with it.

The original architect of this monastery was one *Afonso Domingues*, but the work was taking so long that he had grown old and almost blind. The new architect, David Huguet, believed that a particular abode wouldn't work as originally designed, it seemed too flat, and so he created a new one of his own – except that his creation was destroyed soon after! Time and again he tried to make a new abode, and yet they all failed, one after the other. Eventually *Afonso Domingues* was called back for the job and asked that his original abode be implemented. Although workers were certainly wary of it, they ultimately followed through with the original plan, and when the old design for the abode was finally implemented, *Afonso* stood under it for three whole days, almost chanting "*A abóbada não caiu, a abóbada não cairá!*"[36], after which he died on the spot (due to unrelated causes). The abode he designed, as of today and after over 500 years, is still standing.

So, if you're ever in Portugal and you are near *Batalha* – a town so named after the incidents at *Aljubarrota* – don't forget to visit the *Mosteiro da Batalha*. The abode referenced in this legend is supposedly the one in the Chapter House.

---

name.
36 I.e. "The abode did not fell, the abode will not fall!"

Chapter VI – From the Time of the Explorers (30-35)

From an historical standpoint, chances are that when you think about Portugal, you remember the nautical discoveries and the worldwide empire from the XV and XVI centuries. The same age of travels and discoveries also generated many legends, often retold among sailors or to explain the origins and events connected with some specific places.

30- *Machim* and *Ana D'Arfet*

In the middle of the XIV century lived in England a man whose name in Portuguese[37] is given as *Roberto Machim*. He fell in love with a lady named *Ana D'Arfet*, but her family did not consent to this relationship, instead wanting her to marry someone much richer. So, the two lovers decided to run away to France, but as they were traveling by sea their ship faced a massive storm, which took them far away from their original course. Thus, by mere accident they found themselves in a then-empty island which would later be known as Madeira. *Ana* soon died with a fever, and *Machim* wrote their love story in a wooden cross before he too ended up dying.

When the Portuguese reached Madeira, in the year of 1419, they supposedly found this wooden cross there, with this legend engraved in

---

37 It is likely that all the names present in this legend are corrupted, being Portuguese forms of originally English ones.

it, and ended up naming the area where they disembarked as *Machico*, over that previous traveler.

31- The Statue of the Island of *Corvo*

When the Portuguese reached the island of *Corvo*, in the archipelago of Azores, around 1452, it was completely empty of any human presence. However, a few years later people found in it something truly intriguing – in a place which was specially hard to access there was a statue of a man mounting a horse and pointing somewhere, with some unreadable text, apparently in non-latin characters, under it. A drawing was made, the text was supposedly even copied[38], but when people tried to transport the statue back to Portugal, as it had been ordered by the king *Manuel I*, it was already so extensively damaged that it broke into a thousand pieces – and they were all still taken back to Portugal and placed in the king's room, at some time in the late XV or early XVI centuries, but it is unknown what happened to them afterwards.

Multiple textual sources attest the real existence of this obscure statue, but none of them provide more faithful information than the one described above. And so, chances are that this will always be a mystery for the ages, with a small exception – locals from the island of *Corvo*

---

38 Although there are historical references to this copying, I was ultimately unable to find any real records of the actual text, making it impossible to attempt to find out what was written there.

still say that the place where the statue was found is the *"Ponta do Marco"*[39], so named over the fact it once had such a notable mark in it, and there is also a grotto nearby, which may actually have been the secluded place referred to in this whole legend.

32- *Preste João das Índias*

The legend of Prester John, a powerful christian ruler who lived somewhere in the lands of India, is certainly not exclusive to Portugal, and it may still be fairly famous in many countries around the globe, but an aspect of the whole story appears to be purely from this country. Legend has it that one of the reasons why the Portuguese decided to expand through sea was to locate the legendary lands of *Preste João das Índias* (as he is named here), and multiple sailors even did inquire about him in many of the lands of Africa. Ultimately they always failed to find that legendary empire, once associated with the travels of the apostle Thomas, as they were looking for a ghostly figure, but the fact this legend had a significant impact in portuguese culture deserved to be noted here.

33- *Nau Catrineta*

A famous song and poem from Portugal talks about an adventure related to a possibly legendary *Nau Catrineta*. Essentially, its sailors

---

39 Or "Pontoon of the Mark".

had been lost at sea for multiple days and they ran out of food and drink. In complete desperation, they decided to kill one of the crew members – whether they wanted to eat him too, or simply have less men on board, remains uncertain – and the lot fell to the captain. As his last action, he asked someone to climb to the upper part of the ship and try to spot dry land – and, unexpectedly, the climber did find out they were almost back in Portugal. Quite happy with this outcome, the captain then decided to offer a reward to the discoverer. But, since this whole legend was frequently passed along through oral sources, there are multiple versions of what happened next, two of them being specially famous.

In one version, the spotter explicitly asks for the ship, the *Nau Catrineta*, but the captain states he cannot offer him such a gift, since it actually belongs to the king of Portugal. In another one, the same sailor rejects all potential offers, including this ship, before promptly asking for the captain's soul (because he was actually the Devil in disguise). It is unknown which of these versions came first, if any of the two, but this is particularly interesting because if you go online and try to look up the song – it is fairly easy to find, it goes by the same name as this legend – you may also come across multiple versions of the whole plot. In their essence they're pretty much the same, only a few minor verses usually vary, but the ending may differ significantly, as already presented above.

34- *Adamastor*

The giant *Adamastor* is famous in Portugal through the epic poem of *Luís de Camões*, the *Lusíadas*[40], where he is portrayed as a personification of the Cape of Good Hope. There, the Portuguese have to overcome him in order to later get to India by sea. As such, he is overall remembered by natives as a significant episode of the epic, one they've usually even read back in school, but not as a real legend, since this figure was seemingly invented by the poet with no significant backstory preceding it. However, given the giant's enormous fame in Portuguese culture, you may be able to spot him represented in many places all over Portugal[41], and if you ever go to the *miradouro de Santa Catarina*, in the city of Lisbon, you can even find a particularly notable statue of him there.

35- Enchanted Islands

Although there is not just one specific legend about enchanted islands in Portugal, sailors once imagined there were multiple mysterious islands waiting to be discovered and many strange people living all over the world. From dog-faced men to beings who lived in the dessert and protected themselves from the heat with a giant foot,

---

40 There are multiple translations of this work to English. However, since reading it requires at least some knowledge of Classical Mythology, you may want to get an edition with explanatory notes.
41 The cover art for this book even shows one such representation available in the area of *Buçaco*.

along with islands with sands of pure gold or magically changing locations, there were once many beliefs about strange places and people, most of them only "spotted" by sailors. Nowadays, almost none of those legends subsist, with one notable exception – king *Sebastião*, whose main story was already reported in a previous chapter, is generally thought to be waiting for the time of his return in the *Ilha Encoberta*[42], an island filled with many wonders... exactly what they consist of tend to vary widely from one literary source to another, but in what is arguably the most intriguing of all the portrayals I was able to locate, readers are told that time flows very slowly in the island, that its sands are composed of pure gold dust, and that there are many other people living there with the king, including one *Dom Rodrigo*, alleged to be the last christian ruler of the Iberian Peninsula before the arrival of the Moors, who supposedly escaped there from the Algarve with his bishops and their flock when they saw that the Muslims were coming – a purely christian empire lives in that island and accompanies the king, or so one would think based on this version of its many wonders.

---

42 i.e. "Covered Island". It had this name since a perpetual fog surrounded it, or because king *Sebastião*, under his prophetic title *O Encoberto* (i.e. "the covered one"), lived there.

Chapter VII – Fantastic and Religious Legends (36-41)

In Portugal there is an almost endless number of religious legends, but also a significant number of stories connected with mystical and fantastic elements. To try to cover them all here would be absolutely impossible, there are way over 3000 legends of this kind, but the ones presented here are specially famous ones.

36- The Goat-footed Ladies

In Portugal there are at least two legends associated with a goat-footed lady. The first mentions a really beautiful woman, one *Maria Alva*, who lived in a small castle and once attracted an endless number of suitors, but who refused to marry any of them until someone brought her a pair of shoes she could wear. A certain knight, wishing to fulfill that unusual condition, contacted a local cobbler and asked for his help, but he could not make shoes for someone he had never seen before. And so, the two came up with a plan – with the help of the lady's personal nurse, they decided to spread flour in her room during the night, so that the strange shape of her feet was imprinted on it. The female helper later noticed the shape of the feet and reported it back to the cobbler, who managed to create that unique pair of shoes; as the knight presented *Maria Alva* with them, she felt deeply ashamed over the fact people now knew her deepest secret, and she mysteriously disappeared, never to be seen again, or – according to another version –

threw herself off the tower she lived in.

In another legend, arguably the most famous of these two, a noble was hunting in the forest when he noticed an extremely beautiful woman. He instantly asked her to marry him, and she accepted it under a small condition – he should never again use the sign of the cross in his life[43]. He accepted so, they married and had some children. A few years later, as they were all having dinner, the noble noticed one of his dogs killed another in a dispute for a small piece of meat; shocked over the occurrence, he knocked on a piece of wood thrice, as it is common in Portugal[44], and then accidentally made the sign of the cross. Noticing this holy action, his nameless wife quickly ran away, never to return or be seen ever again.

The village of *Marialva* supposedly got its name over the first of these two women, and a small castle with a tower can still be seen there today. About the second figure, she was mostly used to explain the mysterious origin of a certain family, as its original literary source is a work focusing on the origins and development of many families, the *Livro de Linhagens do Conde D. Pedro*[45]. However, it should also be noted that despite sharing their strange deformity, the two figures

---

43 Although this is never made completely clear in the story, one has to presume she was either the Devil or a demon.
44 According to a local popular belief, this would protect the performer from evil, particularly the kind of evil he just mentioned or thought of.
45 I.e. "The Book of Lineages of the Count *Pedro*". Written in the middle of the XIV century, this work neither seems to exist in modern Portuguese, nor in any English translations.

appear to be completely unrelated.

37- Saint Vincent and Lisbon

Although Saint Vincent supposedly lived in the III century of our era and most natives from Portugal are unaware of his original story (as portrayed by the latin author Prudentius), there is a small legend connecting the saint with the city of Lisbon. Essentially, it says that in the XII century *Afonso Henriques* ordered the bringing of the saint's relics to Lisbon, and so they were fetched from their original location, seemingly in the area of *Sagres*. All the way through the travel by sea the ship was accompanied by two crows[46], and that is why, to this day, the coat of arms of the city of Lisbon presents a ship and two crows. The saint's relics, in case you decide to look for them, were originally taken to what is now named the *Mosteiro de São Vicente de Fora*[47], who was founded at that time, but after the earthquake of 1755 they were taken to the city's See.

38- Fuas Roupinho

Around the year of 1182 *Fuas Roupinho*, a noble and mayor of *Porto de Mós*, was hunting. He spotted a large deer, perhaps the largest

---

46 The presence of these animals can be explained through Saint Vincent's own legend, since they originally protected the body of the deceased saint from any physical harm, until he was – according to the Portuguese version of the story – buried in a church in *Sagres*.

47 This monastery is naturally named over the saint, but the designation "... *de Fora*" comes the fact it was built outside of the city medieval walls.

he had ever seen in his life, and so he decided to chase it. The hunt went on for many hours, and as *Fuas'* horse quickly chased the deer, the hero ended up not noticing they were all approaching a very steep cliff, which would have certainly killed him. About to fall down, in complete desperation he uttered the sacred name of the Virgin Mary, and the horse miraculously stopped in its course, leaving some deep markings in the rock he stood in.

If you go to *Nazaré*, where this whole story took place, you are still be able to spot the famous markings in the rock, and a chapel erected nearby celebrates this whole miracle. Some versions also add a notable element to this whole plot – the deer was not just a regular animal, but actually a transformation of Satan, who had adopted this form in order to test *Fuas Roupinho*'s faith.

39- The Blessing Ring

At one unknown time in his life *Fernando Anes de Lima* saw two weasels defending their burrow from the attack of a snake. After a long battle the weasels were seemingly defeated, but this *Fernando* felt so much compassion for them and their attempt to protect their young that he killed the snake with his sword. Then he went back to his military camp, and some time later he noticed that one of the weasels was coming nearby, with a small precious stone in its mouth. The animal delivered the stone to its savior and quickly went away. So,

Fernando grabbed the strange offer and made a ring with it. Later, he offered it to the family of the *Limas* with his personal blessing, from which the ring obtained its curious name. However, if this mysterious item is still extant today and can be seen somewhere, even after much inquiry I was unable to find its current location.

40- The Enchanted Moors

As mentioned in a previous chapter, Portugal has many legends opposing Moors to Christians. However, across time the Islamic presence in this country became rarer and rarer, and so some of the original legends evolved to include more mystical and fantastic elements. Instead of living Moors, people were now finding enchanted ones, brief remnants of an almost-forgotten past. As such, the "enchanted moor" and the "enchanted *moura*" – the female version seems to be way more common – are figures completely exclusive to the myths and legends of Portugal. There is not just one story associated with them, but there are many all over Portugal, some of them preserved in books and others only extant in oral sources. Overall, these stories tend to follow a set pattern – someone goes to a mysterious place, such as a water stream, an old castle, or a cavern, and they find a very beautiful person of the opposite sex there; they are requested to perform a particular task, following which they are guaranteed a very big reward; the request is attempted, but often failed, leading to the disappearance of the mysterious figure. This failure of the task is generally an important element, since it prevents the existence of physical remains of the occurrence, a very big physical reward, which would otherwise be requested by non-believers.

But the exclusivity to Portugal of these stories has to raise an important question – today, do people still believe in these Enchanted Moors and *Mouras*? Although older people often still remember those stories from their youth, ultimately I was always unable to find even one person who claims to have seen these mystical beings by themselves. Therefore, although the legends containing these figures are indeed exclusive to Portugal, they can now be openly recognized as myths, since nobody appears to believe in them any more.

41- The *Olharapos*, *Olharapas* and *Olhapins*

These three names refer to two different kinds of creatures which were once part of the legends of the north of Portugal. Their stories are almost completely lost today, with the exception of some very subtle pieces of information about them – the *Olharapos* and *Olharapas*, respectively male and female, were members of one same species, could even marry among themselves, were possibly carnivorous, and supposedly had a single eye in their forehead, just like the Cyclops of Ancient Greek Mythology[48]. The *Olhapins* had four or more eyes,

---

48 This comparison is intentional. There are not many extant stories where these creatures intervene, but one such example, preserved by *Ana de Castro Osório*, is very similar to the classical tale of Odysseus and Polyphemus. Whether the stories developed independently, or *Osório*'s tale resulted from adding of the name of *Olharapo* to the

giving them the ability to see everything quite well.

Unfortunately, with the exception of some very vague stories, ones preserved here and there almost by sheer accident, almost nothing else is known about them today.

---

original villain, remains uncertain.

Chapter VIII – Some Famous People and Places (42-52)

In this chapter you'll be able to read some small legends associated with a few famous people and locations from Portugal. Naturally this is not an extensive listing, nor does it cover all the most famous heroes (some of which were already talked about in previous chapters), since almost every small place in this country has some kind of legend associated with it.

42- João Soares de Paiva

João Soares de Paiva is best known as the oldest writer who wrote something in a language which can be vaguely identified as Portuguese. Although others may have actually preceded him, since it is not exactly easy to date such old authors, he is associated with a small legend, according to which the king *Sancho VII* of Navarra – who lived in the XII and XIII centuries – invaded some lands belonging to other monarchs and people, including a few which were actually a property of the poet himself, prompting him to write a poem, which is still extant, about it.

Realistically, there are some other authors and compositions which allege being the oldest written in an early form of Portuguese, such as the *Canção do Figueiral* (alluded to in a previous chapter), but this one is specially noteworthy due to its provable age and association with a small legend.

43- The Rooster of *Barcelos*

To a foreign audience, usually used to seeing a small painted rooster as a significant symbol of Portugal, it could perhaps seem that its originating legend would be a very famous one, but if you were to ask native people about it, most of them would only be able to tell you a partial version of the whole story, if at all. And so, I decided to retell here its most complete version.

Long, long ago, many crimes took place in the city of *Barcelos*[49]. A pilgrim who was traveling to Santiago de Compostela was blamed for all of them, in spite of continuously denying he had done anything wrong. In complete desperation, he asked to see a judge before being taken to the gallows, and this final wish was granted. When they got to the judge's house he was about to have lunch, and pointing to the (dead) rooster in a platter, the pilgrim said that if he was innocent of all the crimes the animal would sing – but it didn't[50]!

And so, the pilgrim was taken to the gallows... he was about to die when the rooster, back at the judge's house, miraculously started to sing, stunning everyone present at the scene. Finally realizing the

---

49 Strangely, if you are to judge the whole occurrence from this story, the real culprit was never caught...

50 If you're already familiar with this legend, you'll notice that the rooster usually sings at this point, and so the pilgrim is quickly forgiven. However, the older version of this legend continued for a bit longer.

pilgrim's innocence, they sent some men to take him back from the gallows, but he would have been dead by then if it wasn't for another strange occurrence – the apostle *Tiago* miraculously appeared on the scene and prevented the hanging of his believer by holding him up. Through these two miracles the pilgrim was saved. And so, many years later he came back to the scene of the hanging and ordered the construction of a monument depicting the whole story.

Today, if you go to *Barcelos* you can see this old monument, attributed to the legendary pilgrim, still there, although its location was changed. It shows Jesus Christ crucified at the top of the scene, followed by a rooster, and the apostle *Tiago* holding up a man about to be hanged, thereby attesting that all these components were really featured in the oldest versions of the legend.

And how did this rooster became a symbol of Portugal? Seemingly, across time he became a famous local pottery theme, associated particularly with the city of Barcelos, and later it was popularized via its presence in international exhibitions, so becoming a cultural icon.

44- *Inês de Castro*

The legend of *Inês* and *Pedro* (who would later become the first king of that name in Portugal[51]), is undoubtedly the most famous love story of Portugal. It reports that when *Pedro* was married to one *Constança Manuel* he fell in love with one of her companions, named *Inês de Castro*. Again and again the two lovers met in secret in the *Quinta das Lágrimas*[52], in *Coimbra*, and when *Constança* died, supposedly of natural causes, supposedly the prince married his beloved in the most complete secret, and they even had three children. However, his father, king *Afonso IV*, never consented or accepted this relationship. In fact, he so much wanted to separate them that he asked for three nobles to kill her – which they did, deeply infuriating his son.

Later, when he finally ascended to the throne and became known as king *Pedro I*, he knew he had some personal promises to fulfill. First, he ordered the execution of the three nobles who had killed his beloved *Inês*. Then, getting her from the grave, he sat her in the throne and asked all his court to treat her as the queen, going as far as requesting that they kiss her hand. And finally, when they both died, they were given lavish graves in the *Mosteiro de Alcobaça*, accompanied by the words "*Até ao fim do mundo*"[53] – believing that everyone will come back to life when the world ends, as Christian Theology generally argues, their graves were even placed one in front of the other, so that they can, at that unique moment, see each other again and once more share their immortal love.

---

51 In fact, in the chapter about legends related to the kings you're able to find two legends related to him.
52 Literally "Estate of Tears", supposedly over the fact the two lovers shed many tears when they met in this place.
53 I.e. "Until the end of the world."

This legend of *Pedro* and *Inês de Castro* has fascinated local audiences for centuries. There are many songs, books, plays and movies about it, some of them better than others, but the kernel of the whole story is the one described here, one still celebrated in the *Quinta das Lágrimas*, the location where the two lovers met so many times, and where *Inês* was later murdered. If you ever go there, you can still see the fountain next to which the two lovers frequently met, but that's about it.

45- *Guiomar Coutinho*

In the XVI century *Guiomar Coutinho*, the sole heiress of two very rich families of nobles, was a very desirable woman. As such, the king *Manuel I* wanted her to marry one of his sons, but the monarch died before the plans were finalized. His successor, king *João III*, attempted to get her to marry his brother, as their common father had desired, but he soon learned a deeply intriguing piece of information – *Guiomar* was supposedly already married to one man named *João de Lencastre*.

She denied the accusation many times, while this supposed husband reaffirmed it as many in return. The case was eventually taken to court and, for now-unknown reasons, it was decided that she could indeed marry *Fernando*, the king's brother, as it had been planned all along. They got married in 1530 and had two children, but in 1534 it all changed for the worse – their second child died at birth, their daughter also died at a very young age, followed by their father, and finally the once very desirable heiress was taken to her grave. And the people considered it was all a curse from God, following what they considered to be *Guiomar*'s potentially illegal marriage.

46- *Pedro Sem*

The man known as *Pedro Sem* probably lived in the early XVI century in the city of *Porto*. He had many local properties and imported many valuable assets from overseas. Then, one day, as he was watching his many ships coming to the local port, he disrespectfully said that not even God himself could make him poor. A few hours later all his ships sank in the *Douro* river; his many houses burned down; and all the gold he stored at his famous tower was stolen. Sooner than later, he fell into the most complete ruin, and could be seen begging through the streets of the city, uttering the phrase *"Dai uma esmola a Pedro Sem, que tudo tinha e agora nada tem"*[54]

Today, his once-famous tower, still known as the *Torre de Pedro Sem*, can still be found in the *Rua da Boa Nova*, in the city of *Porto*, but it was also renovated across the centuries and cannot currently be visited.

---

[54] I.e. "Give some alms to *Pedro Sem*, who once had everything and now has nothing."

47- The Beard of *João de Castro*

João de Castro lived in the first half of the XVI century. He went through many adventures, and at one point in his life he moved to India. He successfully protected the city of Goa against invaders, but later noticed that the fortress of Diu was extensively damaged, and he did not have enough money to repair it. So, what did he do? He wrote a letter to the most eminent citizens of Diu, asking them for a loan, and using his own beard, supposedly the only thing he still had (after having unsuccessfully tried to pawn the bones of one of his children), as collateral. The loan was later granted, but his unusual action, and his beard, became legendary.

In fact, *João de Castro*'s beard became an almost saintly relic, passed from hand to hand across the years, until it finally disappeared from national history. Its current location is unknown. However, in the past it could famously be seen in the *Quinta da Penha Verde*, in *Sintra*, which was once this famous man's property.

48- *"Obras de Santa Engrácia"*

A popular proverb from Portugal alludes to *"obras de Santa Engrácia"*[55] as meaning something which takes a very long time to complete. This comes from the fact that the *Igreja de Santa Engrácia*,

---

55 I.e. "Labours of Saint Engratia".

now best known as the National Pantheon, took almost 300 years to complete. There are many (real) reasons for those delays, but there is also a small legend of a once-famous curse associated with it, which naturally deserves to be recounted here.

In the XVII century there was a small convent near this church. Inside lived a nun who loved a young man very much, and they frequently met in the area. Eventually, his actions were found out when a robbery occurred nearby (which he had nothing to do with), and he was tortured in order to reveal the identity of the nun he loved. And she, in order to help him in his struggle, sent him two melons, along with the phrase "*O calado é o melhor*"[56], as a way to tell him that he should remain quiet. And he did remain quiet, but he was later unjustly condemned to death for the robbery he did not commit. Truly desperate with his fate, with his last gasp he cursed the church that was being built nearby.

And so, if we believe in this whole legend, it was due to a curse that it took almost 300 years for the construction of the church to complete. Now you can visit it, and find some of the most notable people of the nation buried inside of it, but although its top floor provides a noteworthy panoramic view of part of the city, the church itself is, based on popular opinion, far from impressive or worth

---

56 Literally this could mean "The quiet one is the best", but the phrase has a notable double meaning, since a melon "*calado*" is one you've already opened, but a person given the "*calado*" adjective is one that does not talk much.

visiting.

49- The terrain of the *Távoras*

A small part of this legend is famous all across Portugal, but it also carries a small secret with it. According to the historical events, in 1758 the family of the *Távoras* attempted to kill the king *José I*. When their attempted failed, they were hit with very extensive penalties[57], their palace in the area of *Belém* was demolished, and the whole terrain was even salted, so that nothing would grow there until the (metaphorical) end of time. Now, although most local people know about this part of the story, where is this once-famous terrain?

If you go to the area of *Belém*, make your way to the famous store of the *Pastéis de Belém,* then continue walking towards the *Mosteiro dos Jerónimos*, and finally turn on the second path to the right, to a small and strictly pedestrian street. There, you will find a small stone column which attests to the famous events, and some text under it succinctly tells you the story behind it. In fact, the terrain belonging to the family of the *Távoras* stretched almost from the monastery all the way to the *Palácio Nacional de Belém*. Since this terrain was, at the time, almost in front of the river, it was very valuable, and despite the original prohibition, less than 100 years later people were already building new houses in it – and yet, every day

---

57 As mentioned before, their coat of arms was even removed from the Palace of *Sintra*, reducing by one the portrayals available there.

thousands of people walk by this famous street of Lisbon, without ever realizing the legend hidden so close to their location.

50- *Diogo Alves*

Diogo Alves lived in the first half of the XIX century, and despite having actually been born in Spain he is still known as Portugal's most famous and prolific serial killer, supposedly having robbed and thrown over 70 people – including some children, which particularly horrified those who heard of the whole occurrence – from the top of the *Aqueduto das Águas Livres*, in Lisbon. But, as strange as it may sound, he was never caught for any of those repeated crimes – instead, at one point he and a gang he was part of robbed the house of a notable doctor and even killed all its occupants, following which they were all denounced by the young daughter of *Diogo*'s lover, and it was for this specific crime that the serial killer was actually hanged in 1841. It should be noted that the rest of the gang, including the aforementioned lover, were all punished according to their respective roles in the same crime, showing us that his hanging was neither exceptional nor a direct consequence of his previous crimes.

But this story of the so-named *Assassino do Aqueduto*[58] is not completely over yet, and undoubtedly deserves an additional note – his unique case, and his many horrendous actions, fascinated the public and

---

58 I.e. "Killer of the Aqueduct".

the doctors so much that the latter even decided to preserve his head and brain for posterity, and so you can still see it inside a jar in a certain museum in the city of Lisbon, if you're specially curious about how this villain once looked like.

51- *Henriqueta Emília da Conceição e Sousa*

Henriqueta Emília da Conceição e Sousa was born near the mid of the XIX century in the city of Porto. Late – and almost always fictional – reports on her life seem to have added a lot of false details to her real story, but some actual facts about her are still known too – she was an orphan (she never knew her father, and her mother died when she was seven years old), she was raped as a child, and later she dedicated her life to robberies, prostitution and other illegal acts. But she would have been forgotten by now if she was such a mere criminal, and so two crucial aspects stood out in her life – she always dressed up as a man, and she deeply loved a woman named *Teresa Maria de Jesus*, this last element being the one that brought them both fame.

In 1868 *Teresa* died of tuberculosis, and her lover seemingly felt she was unable to live without her. So, she built her what was at the time a lavish grave, and later paid for the whole funeral. Then, in that final day when the coffin was about to be closed for the last time and buried, *Henriqueta* asked to say farewell to her friend in private. This favor was easily granted, and so, when nobody was looking, *Henriqueta* somehow ripped out her former lover's head and took it back to their common house, where she kept it, allegedly even talking to her and kissing her lips, as if the deceased was still among the living. This strange crime was eventually caught by someone and reported back to justice, its perpetrator was even taken to court, but the judges felt she did not deserve to go to jail, hers being seen an act of enormous love from a supposedly crazy woman.

Today, both their graves can still be seen in the *Cemitério do Prado do Repouso*, in the city of Porto, but they were buried eternally apart. People still say *Henriqueta* wanted to be buried alongside with her so-beloved *Teresa*, but it seems that such a request was never granted, for now-unknown reasons.

52- *Teresa Fidago*

The story of *Teresa Fidalgo* is not exactly a legend. It is way more accurate to call it a myth, since it is an extremely new story – it is less than 20 years old – and yet extremely popular online. According to it, this young girl once lived in the area of *Sintra*, but she died in a car crash, and now she roams the empty streets of the same area during the night, asking people for rides and leading them to their own deaths in the same place where she once met her demise.

You may have heard about her from a Portuguese video where she causes the deaths of some young people, or through strange chain messages in social media, but the most important element of her story is the fact that it is all a myth, not a legend or even a real story in any way. Instead, it is simply a fictional story created for a viral video by a film director from Portugal, and it has absolutely no basis in any true events. In fact, before the appearance of his video there was absolutely no significant references to *Teresa Fidalgo* in any literary or oral sources, which easily proves the whole fictionality of the story.

----- THE END -----

A final request – as stated in the preface, this small book was an attempt to bring the most famous portuguese legends to an english-speaking audience. As such, if you have read it and enjoyed it, please write a review about it and share it with other people. Depending exclusively on reader feedback, I could consider writing other books on portuguese legends in the future, but that is entirely up to readers like YOU. Your feedback truly matters!

Printed in Great Britain
by Amazon

33475016R00037